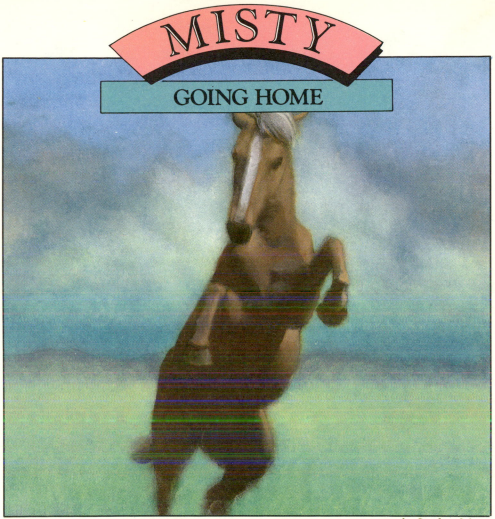

MISTY
GOING HOME

cover by Stephen Moore

from MISTY OF CHINCOTEAGUE by Marguerite Henry
excerpted and adapted by Joan Nichols
illustrated by Steven James Petruccio

CHECKERBOARD PRESS and colophon are trademarks of Macmillan, Inc.

CHILDRENS PRESS CHOICE
A Checkerboard Press/Macmillan title selected for educational distribution
ISBN 0-516-09844-6

The Phantom was the wildest member of the Pied Piper's band. She was also the smartest and most beautiful. Paul and Maureen Beebe first saw her the day they accompanied Grandpa on a visit to Assateague Island. Right from the start they knew they wanted her for their own.

"All the wild ponies here on Assateague are descended from a bunch of shipwrecked Spanish ponies," Grandpa said. "Only the young ones are worth buying, though. Some of the older ones you just can't gentle. Not after they've lived free."

Despite Grandpa's advice, next Pony Penning Day, when the wild ponies were swum across the channel to Chincoteague, Paul and Maureen became the proud owners of the Phantom and of Misty, her brand-new colt.

Right from the start, Misty was happy at Grandpa Beebe's pony ranch on Chincoteague. This was her *home*!

She loved it when Paul or Maureen stroked her neck or brushed her forelock and mane.

The other ponies seemed to enjoy her playfulness.

Sometimes she was wild. Sometimes she was gentle. She loved to gallop across the beach, then stand stock still while a sea gull landed on her back.

Misty was curious! First she nosed the wickie, the soft rope that would go inside her mouth. It tickled and made her sneeze. That was fun! Suddenly, she was wearing it. And it didn't hurt! Not at all. Paul and Maureen sang to her. "Come along, little Misty, come along."

Misty took a few steps forward. That was easy. And for a reward, she got a lump of sugar!

Phantom followed nervously behind. "That's the topsy-turviest pair I ever saw," Grandma said, "the mommy following the colt 'stead of the other way around."

The Phantom was different. It was days before she let anyone touch her. At first she would bolt away, snorting in fright. Only little by little did she learn to accept a human touch.

During the next few months, Paul and Maureen gradually got her used to wearing a band around her middle, first by itself, then with a sack of sand added. After she got used to its weight, she allowed the children to ride her.

Paul and Maureen never made the Phantom wear a bit and bridle. A soft wickie was enough.

"Do you think Phantom is happy?" Maureen asked her brother.

"Of course," Paul answered. "Didn't you see me race her down to the sea this morning. She flew like the wind, snuffing in joy."

"Oh I know she's happy when she runs, but. . . ."

"But what?"

"I often see her standing at the fence with a faraway look in her eyes," Maureen answered.

"I've noticed it too," Paul admitted. "Sometimes I think she's watching the wild ponies playing on the beach at Assateague."

Maureen's face brightened. "But maybe she's really just looking for us," she said hopefully.

"Maybe!" Paul agreed.

One fine spring day, Paul and Maureen were doing their chores. Misty was trotting after them like an overgrown puppy. The Phantom stood apart, looking out to sea.

Paul kept giving the Phantom worried glances. "Let's take turns racing her after our chores are done," he said.

Maureen slipped the wickie rope between the Phantom's teeth. The wild pony trembled with excitement. Maureen jumped on her back.

Paul ran to let the gate down. One leap and the Phantom was over.

Misty tried to follow. "Not today, Misty," Paul said.
He climbed over the fence and stood watching. At last he called out, "My turn now!"

Just as Maureen turned the Phantom over to Paul, a ringing neigh sounded in the distance. Pricking her ears, Phantom jerked her head in the direction of Assateague Island. Another neigh, sharp as a bugle note, pierced the morning stillness.

"It's the Pied Piper!" Grandpa shouted. "He's coming to get the Phantom!"

Paul and Maureen strained
their eyes to see. Sure enough,
the Pied Piper was riding in
with the waves.

"Paul! Get on Phantom's back!" Grandpa called. "Maureen! Get that gate open!"

Maureen took down the bars. She called back to her brother, "Paul! Get a handful of her mane. Ride her toward Misty."

But Paul did not try to
catch the Phantom. Instead,
he removed the wickie.

"Oh, Paul!" screamed Maureen. "Hold her! Hold her! Don't let her go!" The Phantom was whinnying with excitement. Snorting and trumpeting, the Pied Piper swerved around Grandpa, who was trying to head him off.

"Paul!" bellowed Grandpa. "Get out of the way!"

But Paul didn't move.

The Phantom looked at
Paul and hesitated. The
Pied Piper trumpeted again.
Suddenly, as if shaking herself
free, the Phantom twisted her
body high into the air,

whirled past Paul, and ran
to meet the Pied Piper.

Joyously, the two wild
ponies plunged into the surf
and swam across the channel
to their home.

Paul wanted to cry and laugh at the same time. He and Maureen would miss the Phantom, but now she had the freedom she longed for.

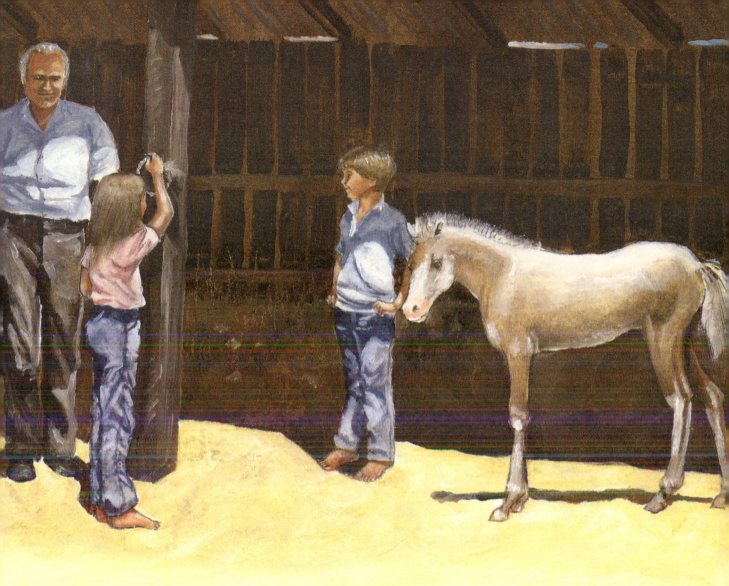

Misty was in the Phantom's stall. She came out and nosed each one's face in turn.

Maureen found a few hairs from the Phantom's tail. She wound them into a circle and fastened them above the manger.

Grandpa's voice was husky. "You did the right thing, children," he said. "Phantom was never really happy here. She belongs to Assateague. But Misty here belongs to us."

Kicking her heels in the air, Misty let out a whinny that sounded like laughter. "Look at me," she seemed to say. "I'm Misty of Chinco-teague!"